Dear Parent:

Congratulations! Your child is taking the first steps on an exciting journey. The destination? Independent reading!

STEP INTO READING® will help your child get there. The program offers books at five levels that accompany children from their first attempts at reading to reading success. Each step includes fun stories, fiction and nonfiction, and colorful art. There are also Step into Reading Sticker Books, Step into Reading Math Readers, and Step into Reading Phonics Readers— a complete literacy program with something to interest every child.

Learning to Read, Step by Step!

Ready to Read   Preschool–Kindergarten
• big type and easy words • rhyme and rhythm • picture clues
For children who know the alphabet and are eager to begin reading.

Reading with Help   Preschool–Grade 1
• basic vocabulary • short sentences • simple stories
For children who recognize familiar words and sound out new words with help.

Reading on Your Own   Grades 1–3
• engaging characters • easy-to-follow plots • popular topics
For children who are ready to read on their own.

Reading Paragraphs   Grades 2–3
• challenging vocabulary • short paragraphs • exciting stories
For newly independent readers who read simple sentences with confidence.

Ready for Chapters   Grades 2–4
• chapters • longer paragraphs • full-color art
For children who want to take the plunge into chapter books but still like colorful pictures.

STEP INTO READING® is designed to give every child a successful reading experience. The grade levels are only guides. Children can progress through the steps at their own speed, developing confidence in their reading, no matter what their grade.

Remember, a lifetime love of reading starts with a single step!

www.stepintoreading.com

Educators and librarians, for a variety of teaching tools, visit us at
www.randomhouse.com/teachers

www.randomhouse.com/kids/disney

Library of Congress Cataloging-in-Publication Data
Gaines, Isabel.
Pooh's honey tree / adapted by Isabel Gaines ; illustrated by Nancy Stevenson.
   p.   cm. — (Step into reading. A step 2 book) SUMMARY: Winnie the Pooh devises a plan to
fool some bees and get honey for his empty tummy.
ISBN 0-7364-1352-9 (trade) — ISBN 0-7364-8013-7 (lib. bdg.)   [1. Teddy bears—Fiction.
2. Honey—Fiction.]   I. Stevenson, Nancy, ill. II. Title. III. Series: Step into reading. Step 2 book.
PZ7.G1277 Poh 2003   [E]—dc21   2002013761

Printed in the United States of America   12 11 10

STEP INTO READING, RANDOM HOUSE, and the Random House colophon are registered trademarks
of Random House, Inc.

DISNEP
Winnie the Pooh

Pooh's Honey Tree

Adapted by Isabel Gaines

Illustrated by Nancy Stevenson

Random House 🏠 New York

Winnie the Pooh
had a big heart.
And a big tummy.

Pooh's big tummy
always looked full.
But it always
felt hungry.

One day Pooh got
out his honeypot.
It was empty!

Pooh heard

a buzzing sound.

BUZZ! BUZZ! BUZZ!

A bee flew past

Pooh's ear.

BUZZ! BUZZ! BUZZ!

Pooh knew that
bees make honey!
So he followed
the bee . . .

. . . into the
Hundred-Acre Wood.

Soon he came
to a tall tree.

Pooh climbed
up the tree.

CRACK!

A branch broke.

Down Pooh fell.

THUMP!

Pooh rubbed his head.
Maybe Christopher Robin
could help Pooh
get some honey.

Pooh set off
to find his friend.

A big blue balloon
was tied to
Christopher Robin's trike.

"May I borrow your
balloon?" asked Pooh.
"I need it to get honey."

"You cannot get honey with a balloon," said Christopher Robin.
"I will use it to float up to the honey," said Pooh.

"Silly old bear," said
Christopher Robin.
"The bees will see you."

Pooh and
Christopher Robin
went back
to the honey tree.

Pooh rolled around
in the mud.

"The bees will think I am
a little black rain cloud,"
said Pooh.

Christopher Robin
sat down
to watch Pooh.

Pooh held on to
the blue balloon.
He floated up to the hole
in the honey tree.

He tried to act like
a little black rain cloud.

Then he reached
into the hole
for some honey.

BUZZ! BUZZ! BUZZ!

The bees began to buzz

around Pooh's head.

Then the
balloon string
came untied.

Pooh hung on to
the balloon.
But the balloon
was losing its air.

Down,
down,
down Pooh fell.

Christopher Robin
put Pooh up on
his shoulders.

"I did not fool
   the bees," said Pooh.
"But I still love honey!"
Christopher Robin
hugged Pooh.
"Silly old bear!"